MW00886867

This book ~~belongs to:~~
is shared with

_____

_____

_____

the missing angels

to all who remember

© October 2024 Conscious Stories LLC
Book 24

Illustrations by Alexis Aronson

Published by
Conscious Stories
350 E. Royal Lane
Suite #150
Irving, TX 75039

www.consciousstories.com

First Edition
Printed in China

ISBN: 978-1-943750-53-5

Library of Congress
Control Number: 2024904786

The last 20 minutes of every day are precious.

Dear parents, teachers, and readers,

As our children grow and navigate the complexities of life, they inevitably face moments of sadness and loss. These experiences, though challenging, are natural parts of the human journey.

Angels are messengers of the Divine, bringing comfort and reassurance. As our children age, the vivid connection to this celestial realm can fade, leaving them feeling as though they have lost a dear friend. In the story "The Missing Angels," we explore how children can find solace, connection and a nurturing sense of peace during these delicate times.

- Like all Conscious Stories, this book begins with the **Snuggle Breathing Meditation**™, a simple mindfulness practice to help you attune and connect more deeply with your children.

- At the end of the story, you will find the **Halo Time** activity page. Connecting intentionally with The Angels will help your kids feel spiritually safe and loved, especially between the ages of 6 and 7 when it's normal to lose connection with their imaginary world

Pro-tip: Safely light a candle and make it a special moment. (Remember to blow it out!)

Enjoy snuggling into togetherness!

Andrew

An easy breathing meditation
Snuggle Breathing

Our story begins with us breathing together.
Say each line aloud and then
take a slow deep breath in and out.

I breathe for me

I breathe for you

I breathe for us

I breathe for all that surrounds us

The Angel Club had been meeting
in the treehouse for two years,
but it didn't feel like home anymore.

"It's not like it used to be," moaned Nimbus.

"I haven't seen **The Angels** since my birthday. Where did they go?"

Just then, the trapdoor swung
open and Mandola climbed
through, neatly dressed as always.

"Hey guys. What are you doing?"

"**The Angels** are hiding
  from Nimbus!" said Gloria.

"Hiding?" exclaimed Mandola.
"I can see them. They are right here."

Nimbus felt left out
as Mandola and Gloria
chatted with **The Angels**.

He wished that he could see
their vibrant, swirling colors
and hear their loving whispers.

Gloria reached out a hand
to comfort Nimbus.

"Archangel Michael says it's normal
to feel the way you do.

Many seven-year-olds forget **The Angels**
and feel alone for a long time.

He is very glad that you
half-remember, and wants to
help you feel more connected."

"He gave us something new
   to teach you," said Mandola excitedly.

"**The Angels** call it Halo Time."

"Close your eyes," said Gloria.
"We're going to take three
   deep breaths together."

15

"Breathing in.
  I want to connect
  with **The Angels**."

"Breathing out.
  Connecting is easy."

17

"Breathing in.
   I want to connect
   with **The Angels**."

"Breathing out.
   Connecting is easy."

"Breathing in.
    I want to connect
    with **The Angels**."

"Breathing out.
    Connecting is easy."

Nimbus felt peaceful as his breath
settled into a steady rhythm.

"Now, focus on the golden ring
above your head." said Gloria.

Nimbus concentrated on his halo
as it spun faster and faster.

After a few quiet moments,
a column of golden light
poured gently down,
all the way to his tender heart.

Nimbus smiled. He recognized the feeling straightaway.

A sweet, syrupy nectar filled his whole body.

A single tear
rolled down his cheek.

His mind fell still.
His heart was warm and cozy.

"It's going to be ok," said Nimbus,
his eyes twinkling
with the lights of heaven.

"I can't see them,
but I can *feel* them!"

"The Angels are
always here!"

> **Trust your angels to catch your wish and bring it to you in a delightfully surprising way.**

Angels are like friends for your heart. They are here to comfort you, support you, and help your heart stay open. Follow the steps and practice asking The Angels for help. They can be there when you need them most.

Meet The Angels

Halo Time

1 **Take 3 breaths**
Breathing in... I want to connect with The Angels
Breathing out... connecting is easy.

2 **Spin your halo**
Focus on your halo while it connects with your heart.

3 **Connect**
Read the 4 Angel Connection mantra's aloud.

4 **Share a wish**
What wish would you like to share with The Angels?

5 **Ask your favorite Angels for help**
Say, "Angels, please help me with my wish."

6 **End with gratitude**
Say, "Thank you, Angels."

I connect with
Archangel Michael
to grow my courage
and strength.

I connect with
Archangel Gabriel
to think clearly and
feel joyful.

I connect with
Archangel Raphael
to heal my body,
heart, and mind.

I connect with
Archangel Uriel
to feel calm, confident,
and happy.

the growing collection

consciousstories

raising mindful kids

the unicorn who found her magic

the hairdresser for unicorns
Andrew Newman & Timea Kulcsar
Illustrated by Liad Bel

the prayer who searched for God
Andrew Newman
Illustrated by Alexis Aronson

the hug factory bursts with love
Andrew Newman
Illustrated by Alexis Aronson

a little light

the forgetful elephant

the girl with waterfall eyes

the sunburnt polar bear
Andrew New
Illustrated by Reda Baly

the missing angels

the boy who searched for silence
Andre

how diablo became Spirit

we are circle people

the tree of goodness

the elephant who tried to tiptoe

Rolling Thunder finds his herd
Andre

the laughing witch

the little brain people
Andrew Ne

the great love of Rose and Thorn

the bee who could not choose her flower
Andrew Newman
Illustrated by Marcella Merois

the hug who got stuck

the fish who searched for water

the dad who didn't know

ellie jumps a mile
Andrew Newman
Illustrated by Lena Ark

the home for sensitive butterflies
Andrew Newman

36

consciousstories

A collection of stories with wise and lovable characters who teach spiritual values to your children

raising mindful kids

Helping you connect more deeply in the last 20 minutes of the day

Stories with purpose

Lovable characters who overcome life's challenges to find peace, love and connection.

Reflective activity pages

Cherish open sharing time with your children at the end of each day.

Simple mindfulness practices

Enjoy easy breathing practices that soften the atmosphere and create deep connection when reading together.

Supportive parenting community

Join a community of conscious parents who seek connection with their children.

Free downloadable coloring pages
Visit www.consciousstories.com

 #ConsciousBedtimeStories   @ConsciousBedtimeStories

37

Andrew Newman is the award-winning author and founder of www.ConsciousStories.com, a growing series of bedtime stories purpose-built to support parent-child connection in the last 20 minutes of the day. His professional background includes deep training in therapeutic healing work and mindfulness. He brings a calm yet playful energy to speaking events and workshops, inviting and encouraging the creativity of his audiences, children K-5, parents, and teachers alike.

Andrew has been an opening speaker for Deepak Chopra, a TEDx presenter in Findhorn, Scotland and author-in-residence at the Bixby School in Boulder, Colorado. He is a graduate of The Barbara Brennan School of Healing, a Non-Dual Kabbalistic healer and has been actively involved in men's work through the Mankind Project since 2006. He counsels parents, helping them to return to their center, so they can be more deeply present with their kids.

TEDx "Why the last 20 minutes of the day matter"

Alexis Aronson — illustrator

Alexis is a self-taught illustrator, designer and artist from Cape Town, South Africa. She has a passion for serving projects with a visionary twist that incorporate image making with the growth of human consciousness for broader impact. Her media range from digital illustration and design to fine art techniques, such as intaglio printmaking, ceramic sculpture, and painting. In between working for clients and creating her own art for exhibition, Alexis is an avid nature lover, swimmer, yogi, hiker, and gardener.

www.alexisaronson.com

I twinkle

stickers
for
sharing

and for your
Star Counter

consciousstories
raising mindful kids

Star Counter

Every time you breathe together and read aloud, you make a star shine in the night sky.

Color in a star to count how many times you have read this book.